ALL BOOKED UP!

written by Janie Mellecker Uhlig and Karri Jesson Ham
illustrated by Priscilla Burris

JANIE MELLECKER UHLIG received a Bachelor of Arts degree and a Master of Arts degree from the University of Northern Colorado. She is an experienced elementary and special education teacher and has taught evening classes for the University of Northern Colorado. She has in-serviced several school districts in the use of learning centers and classroom management. Janie Uhlig is the co-author of a learning centers idea kit.

KARRI JESSON HAM received a Bachelor of Arts degree in elementary education and a Master of Arts degree in reading from the University of Northern Colorado. She is an experienced elementary teacher and has taught several in-services in northern Colorado.

PRISCILLA BURRIS received an Associate of Arts degree in Creative Design from the Fashion Institute of Design and Merchandising in Los Angeles. As a free-lance artist of child-related artwork, she has been drawing since she was one year old. Priscilla lives in southern California.

ISBN 0-933606-43-5

Name _____

Date _____

Title of Book Read: _____

Author: _____

KNOWLEDGE
Name two conflicts that occurred in the story.

_____

_____

_____

_____

_____

_____

_____

_____

COMPREHENSION
Explain one 'sub-adventure' that took place within the adventure story.

_____

_____

_____

_____

_____

_____

_____

APPLICATION
Pretend you are the main character in the story. Write a newspaper ad trying to convince the readers to come with you on your adventure.

_____

_____

_____

_____

_____

_____

_____

_____

Name _____

ANALYSIS
Were the characters in the story prepared for the adventure? If so, how? If not, what could they have done to be more prepared?

_____

_____

_____

_____

_____

_____

_____

_____

SYNTHESIS
Plan another adventure for the characters in the story. Write a summary of the adventure.

_____

_____

_____

_____

_____

_____

_____

_____

EVALUATION
Do you think the adventure in the story was realistic? Support your answer.

_____

_____

_____

_____

_____

_____

_____

_____

Name _____

Date _____

Animals ~ Non-Fiction

Title of Book Read: _____

Author: _____

KNOWLEDGE
List the main animals and what roles they played in the story.

_____

_____

_____

_____

_____

_____

_____

COMPREHENSION
Write a brief description of the animal or animals in the story.

_____

_____

_____

_____

_____

_____

_____

APPLICATION
Pretend the animal in the story is lost. Write a description for the Lost and Found section of a newspaper.

_____

_____

_____

_____

_____

_____

Name _____

ANALYSIS
Would you want the animal in this story for a pet? Explain why or why not.

_____

_____

_____

_____

_____

_____

_____

SYNTHESIS
Write a brief conversation that might take place between two of the animals in the story.

_____

_____

_____

_____

_____

_____

_____

EVALUATION
Do you think the animals in the story were treated humanely? Justify your answer.

_____

_____

_____

_____

_____

_____

Name _____

Date _____

Biography

Title of Book Read: _____

Author: _____

KNOWLEDGE
List five events from the person's life you read about in the order in which they occurred.

_____

_____

_____

_____

_____

_____

COMPREHENSION
Write a short summary of the person's life and explain what specific reasons this person is remembered for.

_____

_____

_____

_____

_____

_____

APPLICATION
Pretend you are the person you read about. Write a diary entry during a special time in your life.

_____

_____

_____

_____

_____

_____

Name _____

ANALYSIS

Would this person have made a good friend? Tell why or why not. What are some qualities a famous person possesses?

_____

_____

_____

_____

_____

_____

_____

SYNTHESIS

What if the person you read about lived 30 years in the future? Write about the kinds of things he/she might contribute to society in the future.

_____

_____

_____

_____

_____

_____

_____

EVALUATION

Do you think a biography should have been written about this person? Explain.

_____

_____

_____

_____

_____

_____

_____

Challenges In Life

Title of Book Read: _____

Author: _____

KNOWLEDGE
What kind of challenge did the main character or characters face in the story?

_____

_____

_____

_____

_____

_____

_____

_____

COMPREHENSION
Explain how this challenge affected the character or characters.

_____

_____

_____

_____

_____

_____

APPLICATION
Pretend you are the main character in the story. Write a letter to a 'Dear Abby' person about one of your problems.

_____

_____

_____

_____

_____

_____

_____

Name_____

ANALYSIS
Write a short letter to the author explaining what kind of insights you gained by reading this book.

_____

_____

_____

_____

_____

_____

_____

SYNTHESIS
Write a short poem expressing the main character's feelings.

_____

_____

_____

_____

_____

_____

_____

EVALUATION
Do you think it is wise for children to read about 'real life' situations? Explain why or why not.

_____

_____

_____

_____

_____

_____

Name _____

Date _____

Choose Your Own Adventure

Title of Book Read: _____

Author: _____

KNOWLEDGE
List the main characters in one of the stories and write an adjective to describe each one.

_____

_____

_____

_____

_____

_____

_____

COMPREHENSION
Select one of the stories and write five main events in sequential order.

_____

_____

_____

_____

_____

_____

APPLICATION
Pretend you are one of the characters in the story. Write five things you feel would be necessary to take with you on the adventure.

_____

_____

_____

_____

_____

_____

ANALYSIS
Compare two of the endings in the book. How are they alike and different?

_____

_____

_____

_____

_____

_____

_____

_____

SYNTHESIS
There are many different endings to the book. Write a paragraph explaining how you would change one of the endings.

_____

_____

_____

_____

_____

_____

_____

EVALUATION
Which was your favorite story? Explain your answer.

_____

_____

_____

_____

_____

_____

_____

Death, Grief, Or Loss

Title of Book Read: _____

Author: _____

KNOWLEDGE
What is the setting of the story?

_____

_____

_____

_____

_____

_____

COMPREHENSION
Explain how you think the family and friends of the deceased character felt after the death. Describe their emotions.

_____

_____

_____

_____

_____

_____

APPLICATION
Write a short news article about the death of the character in the story. Include the who, what, when, and where.

_____

_____

_____

_____

_____

_____

ANALYSIS
What kinds of stages did the character in the story go through in dealing with death?

_____

_____

_____

_____

_____

_____

_____

SYNTHESIS
Pretend you are asked to say a few words at the funeral of the deceased character. You want to let everyone know what kind of person he/she was. Write a brief speech you would give.

_____

_____

_____

_____

_____

_____

_____

EVALUATION
Think back over the story. What part of the story affected you the most? Tell what happened in that part and how you felt.

_____

_____

_____

_____

_____

_____

_____

Fables

Title of Book Read: _____

Author: _____

KNOWLEDGE
Make a list of the animals which appear in this fable.

_____

_____

_____

_____

_____

_____

_____

COMPREHENSION
What do you see as the 'lesson to be learned' in this fable? Use your own words to explain the moral at the end of the fable.

_____

_____

_____

_____

_____

_____

_____

APPLICATION
Make a list of common sayings and phrases which come from fables.

_____

_____

_____

_____

_____

_____

_____

_____

Name _____

ANALYSIS
Examine the use of *personification* and describe how it is used in this fable.

_____

_____

_____

_____

_____

_____

_____

SYNTHESIS
Choose a favorite character in the story and write a series of interview questions for a talk show with you as the host.

_____

_____

_____

_____

_____

_____

_____

EVALUATION
Do you feel the moral to the story has importance to your life? Explain.

_____

_____

_____

_____

_____

_____

_____

Name _____

Date _____

Fairy Tales

Title of Book Read: _____

Author: _____

KNOWLEDGE

Fairy tales are forms of folk tales, and since they have been passed down by 'the folks', we don't really know who originally authored them. Who is given credit for the fairy tale you read and where did the tale originate?

_____

_____

_____

_____

_____

_____

_____

COMPREHENSION

In fairy tales, the characters are either altogether good or altogether bad, and they seldom change during the story. Identify the good characters and bad characters in your tale and explain the characteristics which make them so.

_____

_____

_____

_____

_____

_____

APPLICATION

The events in fairy tales stand out among folk tales because of the magical quality of the happenings. Describe an event in your life around which you could use a fairy godmother's or an elf's help in solving.

_____

_____

_____

_____

_____

_____

Name _____

ANALYSIS
Certain similarities seem to occur in fairy tales. There is often: 1) a struggle between good and evil, 2) the little guy outwitting the big guy, and 3) a long journey of trials in life with happiness the end result. Using these three categories, list the elements of your tale.

_____

_____

_____

_____

_____

_____

_____

_____

SYNTHESIS
Take the villain's point of view and tell how he or she feels about what happened.

_____

_____

_____

_____

_____

_____

_____

_____

EVALUATION
Write a short statement to support the good and bad in three main characters. Then decide which character is your favorite and explain your reasons.

_____

_____

_____

_____

_____

_____

  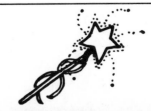

Name _____

Date _____

Fantasy

Title of Book Read: _____

Author: _____

KNOWLEDGE
List the main characters and any descriptions provided by the author.

_____

_____

_____

_____

_____

_____

_____

COMPREHENSION
Fantasy in literature can be set in the real world with unreal occurrences (low fantasy) or in another world (high fantasy). Describe the setting for your novel using these terms.

_____

_____

_____

_____

_____

_____

_____

APPLICATION
Put the plot into six sequential sentences.

_____

_____

_____

_____

_____

_____

_____

Name _____

ANALYSIS
Explain what could and could not have happened in the story.

_____

_____

_____

_____

_____

_____

_____

SYNTHESIS
How could you write yourself into the fantasy? What role would you wish to play?

_____

_____

_____

_____

_____

_____

_____

EVALUATION
List three reasons you enjoy or do not enjoy reading fantasy. Explain.

_____

_____

_____

_____

_____

Name _____

Date _____

Folk Tales

Title of Book Read: _____

Author: _____

KNOWLEDGE

Make a list of the main characters and a term from the story which describes each one.

_____

_____

_____

_____

_____

_____

_____

COMPREHENSION

Categorize the characters in terms of good vs. evil.

_____

_____

_____

_____

_____

_____

_____

_____

APPLICATION

Pretend you are going to entertain one of the characters for a day. Who would you entertain and what would you do together?

_____

_____

_____

_____

_____

_____

_____

Name _____

ANALYSIS

Folk tales repeatedly make use of the numbers three and seven. Analyze this tale to find examples of the numbers.

_____

_____

_____

_____

_____

_____

_____

_____

SYNTHESIS

Write a newspaper headline for the story.

_____

_____

_____

_____

_____

_____

_____

_____

EVALUATION

Tell what human values or ideas are supported in the story and how they relate to your life.

_____

_____

_____

_____

_____

_____

_____

Generic Questions ~ (Free Choice!)

Title of Book Read: _____

Author: _____

KNOWLEDGE
List five major events in the story in chronological order.

_____

_____

_____

_____

_____

_____

_____

_____

COMPREHENSION
Find five adjectives in the story that helped create the mood.

_____

_____

_____

_____

_____

_____

_____

_____

APPLICATION
Write an advertisement to entice someone else to read the book.

_____

_____

_____

_____

_____

_____

_____

Name _____

ANALYSIS
Compare the way the character thinks and acts at the beginning of the story with the way he or she thinks and acts at the end.

_____

_____

_____

_____

_____

_____

_____

_____

SYNTHESIS
Write a new ending to the story.

_____

_____

_____

_____

_____

_____

_____

EVALUATION
Did you like or dislike this story? Explain your answer.

_____

_____

_____

_____

_____

_____

Generic Questions ~ (Free Choice!)

Title of Book Read: _____

Author: _____

KNOWLEDGE

List the who, what, when and where of the story.

_____

_____

_____

_____

_____

_____

_____

COMPREHENSION

Describe in detail the setting of the book.

_____

_____

_____

_____

_____

_____

_____

APPLICATION

Write three facts and three opinions from the story.

_____

_____

_____

_____

_____

_____

ANALYSIS
Would the main character make a good friend? Tell why or why not.

_____

_____

_____

_____

_____

_____

_____

SYNTHESIS
Pretend you are talking on the phone to the main character in the story. Write the dialogue for your telephone conversation.

_____

_____

_____

_____

_____

_____

_____

_____

EVALUATION
Do you think the main character in the story acted appropriately? Justify your answer.

_____

_____

_____

_____

_____

_____

_____

Name _____

Date _____

Handicaps

Title of Book Read: _____

Author: _____

KNOWLEDGE
Name one conflict that happened to the main character. Also, list three things the handicapped person in the story used to make his/her life easier.

_____

_____

_____

_____

_____

_____

COMPREHENSION
Choose (a) or (b). Circle the letter you are answering.
(a) Write a paragraph describing why the author chose this particular title for the book.
(b) Write a short summary of the story.

_____

_____

_____

_____

_____

_____

APPLICATION
Research the handicap discussed in the story and write a paragraph about the handicap.

_____

_____

_____

_____

_____

_____

Name _____

ANALYSIS
What are some ways the character in the story compensated for being handicapped?

_____

_____

_____

_____

_____

_____

_____

SYNTHESIS
Pretend the character in the story had a different handicap. Tell what the handicap was and how it might effect the plot.

_____

_____

_____

_____

_____

_____

_____

_____

EVALUATION
You are a taxpayer and you are being asked to pay higher taxes to support a school for the handicapped. Will you support the tax or fight it? Support your position.

_____

_____

_____

_____

_____

_____

Historical Fiction

Title of Book Read: _____

Author: _____

KNOWLEDGE
Which historical character or what historical event is the focus for this novel?

_____

_____

_____

_____

_____

_____

COMPREHENSION
Describe the time and setting for the novel.

_____

_____

_____

_____

_____

_____

APPLICATION
Using the information from the book, write five headings that could be used in a history textbook.

_____

_____

_____

_____

_____

_____

_____

Name _____

ANALYSIS
Describe the impact or role this character and/or event has had on society.

_____

_____

_____

_____

_____

_____

_____

SYNTHESIS
Choose one of the human conflicts described in the story and write a change in the event which would alter the course of history.

_____

_____

_____

_____

_____

_____

_____

EVALUATION
Write a newspaper or television review of the book stating your opinions regarding the overall quality of the story. Explain your reasoning.

_____

_____

_____

_____

_____

_____

_____

Name _____

Date _____

How-To...

Title of Book Read: _____

Author: _____

KNOWLEDGE

List four facts you learned from reading this book.

_____

_____

_____

_____

_____

_____

_____

_____

COMPREHENSION

Describe in detail one aspect of the book that will be helpful to you.

_____

_____

_____

_____

_____

_____

_____

APPLICATION

You have been asked to write an original 'how to' book. Write a title and list the topics and headings you will include in your book.

_____

_____

_____

_____

_____

_____

_____

Name _____

ANALYSIS
Make an 8-10 step 'how to' chart of a procedure you learned about in the book you read.

_____

_____

_____

_____

_____

_____

_____

_____

SYNTHESIS
Imagine that you were asked to improve the book. Explain your ideas for improvement.

_____

_____

_____

_____

_____

_____

_____

_____

EVALUATION
Was it beneficial for you to read this book? Why or why not?

_____

_____

_____

_____

_____

_____

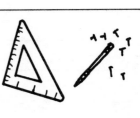

Name _____

Date _____

 Humor

Title of Book Read: _____

Author: _____

KNOWLEDGE
List the main characters in the story and one word to describe each character.

_____

_____

_____

_____

_____

_____

_____

COMPREHENSION
Describe one humorous event that occurred in the story and tell why you thought it was funny.

_____

_____

_____

_____

_____

_____

_____

APPLICATION
Make a short cartoon about a funny event that occurred in the story.

_____

_____

_____

_____

_____

_____

_____

Name _____

ANALYSIS
What kinds of situations make this story humorous?

_____

_____

_____

_____

_____

_____

_____

SYNTHESIS
Write another short humorous episode for the story which might have happened to the main character.

_____

_____

_____

_____

_____

_____

_____

_____

EVALUATION
Write a brief note to the author of the book explaining why you liked the story.

_____

_____

_____

_____

_____

_____

_____

Mother Goose or Poetry

Title of Book Read: _____

Author: _____

KNOWLEDGE
List your favorite character in this collection and tell the role the character played in the selection.

_____

_____

_____

_____

_____

_____

_____

_____

COMPREHENSION
Describe the setting of one of your favorite selections.

_____

_____

_____

_____

_____

_____

_____

APPLICATION
Write five cause and effect situations from the selection.

_____

_____

_____

_____

_____

_____

_____

_____

Name _____

ANALYSIS
Why do you feel this collection of material was considered worthwhile enough to be published?

_____

_____

_____

_____

_____

_____

_____

SYNTHESIS
Choose one of the selections and write a TV news flash as if it had really happened.

_____

_____

_____

_____

_____

_____

_____

EVALUATION
Categorize your favorites and tell what emotion each brings to you, the reader (i.e. happiness, sadness, fear, etc.).

_____

_____

_____

_____

_____

_____

Name _____

Date _____

Title of Book Read: _____

Author: _____

KNOWLEDGE
Who was the detective in the story? List three words to describe the detective.

_____

_____

_____

_____

_____

_____

_____

COMPREHENSION
List the conflicts in the story and tell how they were resolved.

_____

_____

_____

_____

_____

_____

_____

APPLICATION
Look up fingerprinting and write a paragraph explaining how fingerprints can be valuable to a detective's case.

_____

_____

_____

_____

_____

_____

_____

Name _____

ANALYSIS
Make a sequential list of events which affected the solution of the mystery.

_____

_____

_____

_____

_____

_____

_____

_____

SYNTHESIS
Write another short episode to the mystery story.

_____

_____

_____

_____

_____

_____

_____

_____

EVALUATION
Most mysteries include some of the following elements: crime, suspense, detective, alibi, and clues. Evaluate the mystery you have read on three of these elements.

_____

_____

_____

_____

_____

_____

_____

Name _____

Date _____

Myths

Title of Book Read: _____

Author: _____

KNOWLEDGE
List the main characters, both mortal and gods.

_____

_____

_____

_____

_____

_____

_____

COMPREHENSION
Describe the natural occurrence for which a pre-scientific explanation is made.

_____

_____

_____

_____

_____

_____

_____

APPLICATION
Make a list of the Greek names and the mythological character for which each stands.
(Extra credit if you can also list Roman names for each!)

_____

_____

_____

_____

_____

_____

_____

Name _____

ANALYSIS
What aspects of this story helped to create the mood?

_____

_____

_____

_____

_____

_____

_____

_____

SYNTHESIS
Compose a diary page about the hero's or heroine's feelings.

_____

_____

_____

_____

_____

_____

_____

_____

EVALUATION
What did you find most fascinating about this myth?

_____

_____

_____

_____

_____

_____

_____

Non-Fiction

Title of Book Read: _____

Author: _____

KNOWLEDGE
List five facts you learned from the book.

_____

_____

_____

_____

_____

_____

_____

_____

COMPREHENSION
Pick something from the story that you think is interesting. Write a paragraph explaining it.

_____

_____

_____

_____

_____

_____

_____

_____

APPLICATION
Write a short 'teaser' that would encourage someone else to read the book.

_____

_____

_____

_____

_____

_____

Name _____

ANALYSIS
Do you think the title was appropriate for the book? Tell why or why not.

_____

_____

_____

_____

_____

_____

_____

SYNTHESIS
Create five trivia questions relating to the topic you read about. Be sure to include the answers!

_____

_____

_____

_____

_____

_____

_____

_____

EVALUATION
Would you recommend others read this book? Tell why or why not.

_____

_____

_____

_____

_____

_____

Science Fiction

Title of Book Read: _____

Author: _____

KNOWLEDGE

Name one conflict in the story. Also, make a list of the futuristic characters and events found in this novel, i.e. aliens, time travel, etc.

_____

_____

_____

_____

_____

_____

_____

_____

COMPREHENSION

Write five sentences in sequence to describe the main events.

_____

_____

_____

_____

_____

_____

_____

_____

APPLICATION

Write a news article about the most exciting or dangerous part of the story.

_____

_____

_____

_____

_____

_____

_____

Name _____

ANALYSIS
Why is this novel considered science fiction? How is it different from an adventure novel?

_____

_____

_____

_____

_____

_____

_____

SYNTHESIS
Create something in your mind that would be of use to the characters in the story. Describe in detail what your creation is and why it would be useful.

_____

_____

_____

_____

_____

_____

_____

EVALUATION
Do you think any part of this story could really happen in future years? Describe a part of the story you think could or could not happen and explain your reasoning.

_____

_____

_____

_____

_____

_____

Name _____

Date _____

Title of Book Read: _____

Author: _____

KNOWLEDGE
Choose either a sport or an athlete from your book and list three interesting questions and answers for a sports trivia contest.

_____

_____

_____

_____

_____

_____

_____

_____

COMPREHENSION
Describe the main focus or format used in this book.

_____

_____

_____

_____

_____

_____

_____

APPLICATION
Apply what you know about health and sports to explain the need for an athlete to take care of his/her body.

_____

_____

_____

_____

_____

_____

_____

Name _____

ANALYSIS
Analyze the special requirements necessary to be a world class athlete and make a schedule of one typical day in the athlete's life.

_____

_____

_____

_____

_____

_____

_____

SYNTHESIS
Imagine yourself as the "STAR"! Describe your sport, your training, and your accomplishment.

_____

_____

_____

_____

_____

_____

_____

EVALUATION
Evaluate the high salaries famous athletes are paid and decide whether you think it is right or wrong for a sports figure to get that amount for his/her salary.

_____

_____

_____

_____

_____

_____

_____

Stories from Other Lands

Title of Book Read: _____

Author: _____

KNOWLEDGE
Name one problem the main character faced in the story. Tell how it was resolved.

_____

_____

_____

_____

_____

_____

_____

_____

COMPREHENSION
Describe the setting of the story in detail.

_____

_____

_____

_____

_____

_____

_____

APPLICATION
Look up information on the country where the story took place. Pretend you are the main character in the book and write a short letter to someone encouraging him or her to visit your country.

_____

_____

_____

_____

_____

_____

_____

Name _____

ANALYSIS
What are some things you would see in the country you read about that you would not see in your own country?

_____

_____

_____

_____

_____

_____

_____

SYNTHESIS
How would the story change if the setting had been in your country? Write about how you think it would be different.

_____

_____

_____

_____

_____

_____

_____

EVALUATION
Do you think you would enjoy living where the story took place? Why or why not? (Be sure to evaluate geography, climate, customs, etc.)

_____

_____

_____

_____

_____

_____

Name _____

Date _____

Title of Book Read: _____

Author: _____

KNOWLEDGE
Who is the hero?

_____

_____

_____

_____

_____

_____

_____

COMPREHENSION
Describe the region of the country in which this tall tale is set.

_____

_____

_____

_____

_____

_____

_____

APPLICATION
Make a list of the clothing the hero would purchase in a department store today. Be sure to think about the styles your hero might adopt for his/her personality.

_____

_____

_____

_____

_____

_____

_____

Name _____

ANALYSIS

Why do you think a society creates these 'bigger than life' heroes?

_____

_____

_____

_____

_____

_____

_____

SYNTHESIS

Imagine someone you know and make him/her into a hero or heroine in a tall tale.
What would your tall tale be titled?

_____

_____

_____

_____

_____

_____

_____

EVALUATION

Make a list of the exaggerations used in the tale and tell why each did or did not add to the story.

_____

_____

_____

_____

_____

_____

_____

Name _____

Date _____

A Textbook Chapter

Title of Book Read: _____

Author: _____

KNOWLEDGE

Make a list of the subtitles and write any details necessary to explain the major concepts for each.

_____

_____

_____

_____

_____

_____

_____

_____

COMPREHENSION

Write a short summary of one of the main ideas presented in this chapter.

_____

_____

_____

_____

_____

_____

_____

_____

APPLICATION

Write an alternate title for this chapter.

_____

_____

_____

_____

_____

_____

_____

ANALYSIS
Decide upon five concepts which you think are important enough for a test on this chapter.

_____

_____

_____

_____

_____

_____

_____

_____

SYNTHESIS
Design a test using your five concepts from the previous task.

_____

_____

_____

_____

_____

_____

_____

_____

EVALUATION
Do you think this chapter was easy to understand? Explain why.

_____

_____

_____

_____

_____

_____

_____

Name _____

Date _____

Wordless Books

Title of Book Read: _____

Author: _____

KNOWLEDGE
Describe one of the characters from the illustrations. Share with another student to see if your character can be identified.

_____

_____

_____

_____

_____

_____

_____

_____

COMPREHENSION
Explain the plot of the story.

_____

_____

_____

_____

_____

_____

_____

APPLICATION
Write some text to go with one of the illustrations. List the page of the illustration.

_____

_____

_____

_____

_____

_____

_____

_____

Name _____

ANALYSIS
Why do you think the author chose to use no text? How does this technique affect the story?

_____

_____

_____

_____

_____

_____

_____

SYNTHESIS
Describe the subject you would choose to create in a wordless book.

_____

_____

_____

_____

_____

_____

_____

EVALUATION
Do you think it is valuable to create wordless books? Tell why or why not.

_____

_____

_____

_____

_____

_____

The Conflict in a Novel

Title of Book Read: _____

Author: _____

KNOWLEDGE
List at least two problems or conflicts found in this story.

_____

_____

_____

_____

_____

_____

_____

_____

COMPREHENSION
Describe the solutions the author chose for the above conflicts.

_____

_____

_____

_____

_____

_____

_____

APPLICATION
Describe one conflict a person your age might encounter for each of the major conflict types:
1. Man vs. Man 2.   Man vs. Himself 3.   Man vs. Society 4.   Man vs. Nature

_____

_____

_____

_____

_____

_____

_____

ANALYSIS

Choose one of the major conflicts in this story and analyze at least two solutions you can think of. Describe the consequences of each.

_____

_____

_____

_____

_____

_____

_____

_____

SYNTHESIS

Many stories have no final resolution in order to allow for the creation of a sequel to the story. Create one more conflict for your main character, leaving the reader wondering what the outcome will be.

_____

_____

_____

_____

_____

_____

_____

EVALUATION

Choose one of the major conflicts and evaluate the solution the author chose for it. Explain your feelings.

_____

_____

_____

_____

_____

_____

_____